W9-BYF-615

Look and Find®

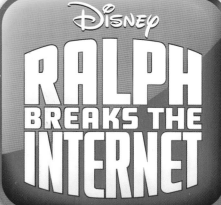

Disney

RALPH BREAKS THE INTERNET

we make books come alive™

pi kids® **Phoenix International Publications, Inc.**

Chicago · London · New York · Hamburg · Mexico City · Paris · Sydney

BEEP-BEEP-BEEP! That sound means a new game has been plugged in at Litwak's arcade! Vanellope von Schweetz hopes it's a new racing game—she knows all the tracks in *Sugar Rush* by heart. But *WiFi* isn't a game, it's the Internet...whatever that is.

While Wreck-It Ralph tries to pronounce *WiFi*, say hello to these characters from all over the arcade:

Calhoun

Zombie

Vanellope

Sour Bill

Gene

Surge

Felix

Ralph

Vanellope's game, *Sugar Rush*, needs a new steering wheel. The only place to get one is from eBay. Ralph and Vanellope are going to the Internet! On the busy Internet streets, they look for someone who can give them directions. KnowsMore seems like a helpful fellow!

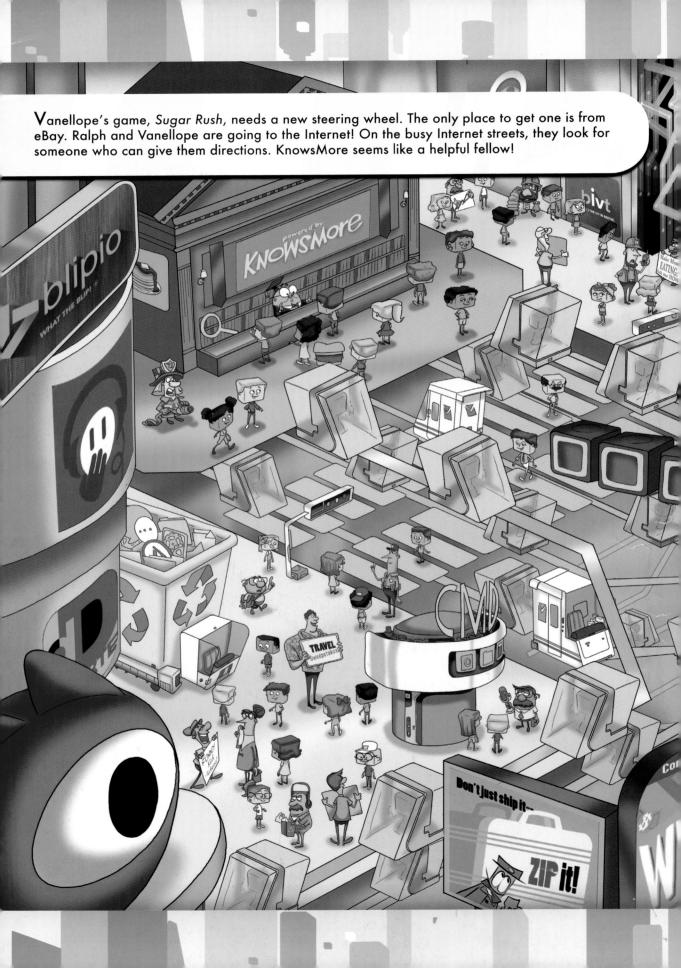

Help Vanellope and Ralph figure out these pop-ups, cookies, and other pieces of Internet infrastructure:

this pop-up	cookies	recycle bin	KnowsMore	this pop-up	e-mail truck

Oh, boy! At eBay, Ralph and Vanellope find aisles and aisles of stuff. To them, it seems like a game, and all you need to do is shout the biggest number. At the last second, Ralph shouts *twenty-seven-thousand-and-one*...and wins!

Find these rare items the friends pass by on their way to collect the steering wheel:

haunted sandwich | Bigfoot autographed photo | seven-leafed clover | upside-down postage stamp | brick race car | imaginary friend | sloth-shaped potato chip | sorrowful kitten painting

It turns out that Ralph's winning number represents money. Now Ralph and Vanellope need to pay $27,001 for the steering wheel! At JP Spamley's, the friends learn how to get rich by playing video games. All they need to do is find certain game items, and then a person in the real world will pay them.

ARE YOU PAYING TOO MUCH?
Take advantage of this special offer!
Click Here

"MY SISTER IN-LAW GOT RICH$$ PLAYING VIDEO GAMES!!!"

GET STARTED TODAY!
LEETStreet

START COLLECTING LOOT TODAY!

$5
WANTED
Platinum Spade

WANTED:
Homunculus Hammer
$4

Wizard's W

WANTED
Rainbow Gobstopper
$5
Chocolate Challenge

While Spamley explains his system, check out these valuable items:

gumdrop

this sword

suit of armor

gem

rutabagas

giant's purse

treasure chest

The highest dollar item on Spamley's list is Shank's car from *Slaughter Race*. The game is a shark-eat-dog world of missile explosions, trash fires, and creepy clowns. Vanellope feels like she has found a new home! Ralph, on the other hand, is ready to go back to Litwak's.

Help Ralph and Vanellope sneak around Shank and her gang:

Felony

Pyro

Debbie

Butcher Boy

Shank

Meanwhile, Fix-It Felix and Sergeant Calhoun have taken in the other displaced drivers of *Sugar Rush*. Looking around the dinner table, Calhoun realizes that leading a combat platoon is easy compared to parenting pre-teens! Have they bitten off more than they can chew?

Help the overwhelmed caregivers by keeping an eye on these racers:

Adorabeezle
Winterpop

Crumbelina
DiCaramello

Taffyta
Muttonfudge

Rancis
Fluggerbutter

Snowanna
Rainbeau

Jubileena
Bing-Bing

Back in the Internet, Ralph and Vanellope have discovered they can make more money by making silly videos called memes. With the help of Yesss, the master of all things trending and head algorithm at BuzzzTube, Ralph's memes could be big—like, break-the-Internet big.

Scroll through BuzzzTube and "like" these other trending videos:

A virus has cloned Ralph, and the clones are breaking the Internet! This isn't what Yesss had in mind. Like regular Ralph, the clones are worried that Vanellope is abandoning them because she has decided to stay in *Slaughter Race*. But Vanellope would never do that. No matter where she is, Ralph will always be Vanellope's best friend.

Help reassure these clones that their bestie isn't going anywhere:

Litwak's Family Fun Center is home to arcade games, old and new. Head back to Game Central Station and collect these game items—no quarters required!

mug of root beer

potion

coin

cherries

wooden sword

turkey leg

key

Scroll back to the Internet streets and search for these helpful Netizens:

security

HTML construction worker

e-mail carrier

finder

recycler

pop-up blocker

Do I hear three-and-a-quarter? Click back to eBay and try to outbid these "players":

Need to make a little moola? Meander back to Spamley's and grab these fliers:

There's no place like *Slaughter Race*! Throw it in reverse and steer around these unique *Slaughter Race* things:

stolen refrigerator

clown

sewer shark

this mace

pigeon

this car

trash fire

Race back to Felix and Calhoun's apartment and find 20 medals from *Fix-It Felix, Jr.*

It's Caturday! Browse back to BuzzzTube and find videos starring these photogenic felines:

Some of the Ralph copies didn't turn out quite right. Return to the clones and find these irregular Ralphs:

Congratulations, you've unlocked the bonus level! Go back and find a plate of pancakes and a milkshake in each scene.